**CUMBRIA COUNTY LIBRARY**

3 8003 0

KT-434-864

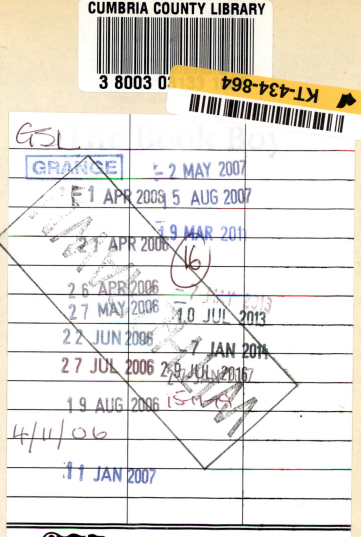

GSL

GRANGE    2 MAY 2007

F 1 APR 2008 5 AUG 2007

19 MAR 2011

21 APR 2006

26 APR 2006

27 MAY 2006   10 JUL 2013

22 JUN 2006   7 JAN 2014

27 JUL 2006   29 JUL 2016

19 AUG 2006

4/11/06

11 JAN 2007

**Cumbria Library Services**

COUNTY COUNCIL

This book is due for return on or before the last date above.
It may be renewed by personal application, post or telephone,
if not in demand.

C.L. 18F

# The Book Boy

Joanna Trollope

Bloomsbury

**CUMBRIA COUNTY LIBRARY**

| HJ | 01/04/2006 |
|----|------------|
| TRO | £2.99 |

First published in Great Britain 2006

Copyright © 2006 by Joanna Trollope

The moral right of the author has been asserted

Bloomsbury Publishing Plc, 36 Soho Square, London W1D 3QY

A CIP catalogue record for this book is available
from the British Library

ISBN 0 7475 8211 4
9780747582113

10 9 8 7 6 5 4 3 2 1

Set in Stone Serif

Typeset by SX Composing DTP, Rayleigh, Essex
Printed in Great Britain by Clays Ltd, St Ives plc

All papers used by Bloomsbury Publishing are natural,
recyclable products made from wood grown in well-managed
forests. The manufacturing processes conform to the
environmental regulations of the country of origin.

www.joannatrollope.com

# CHAPTER ONE

ALICE WOKE EARLY. She always woke early. Always had. Long ago, because of the babies. Now, when the babies were grown up, out of habit. She woke early and lay there, very, very still.

Ed didn't like it if she moved. He didn't like it if she got up, either. He grunted, if she moved. And if she got up, he'd say, 'Stop that!'

'Stop what?' she'd say.

'Stop waking me up.'

'But you are awake,' she'd say. 'And it's morning.'

That made him cross. If she told him it was morning, that made him cross, and then the start to the day was spoilt.

'Alice,' her friend Liz said, 'don't let that man bully you.'

Liz knew about Alice. She knew about Ed, too. Often, she tried to help Alice, but Alice was difficult to help.

'He doesn't,' Alice said.

But he did. He bullied Alice the way her father had bullied her mother. And both men, Alice thought, had an excuse to bully. After all, Alice shared her mother's secret. They both had – didn't they? – the same secret.

It had never struck Alice, as a child, that her father might have helped with her secret. Or her mother's. It didn't strike her that Ed might have helped her, as a woman. Or that her mother might have done something to help. The secret was just one of those things. Like frizzy hair or fat ankles. You had to live with it.

She turned her head. Ed's big body was turned away from her. His body was like a big dark hill against the dim light.

Alice would know the shape of Ed anywhere. She was good at shapes. If you were no good at words you got good at shapes. Shapes of people. Shapes of words. Sometimes, Alice could read a word because she knew its shape.

'Stop that,' Ed said, all of a sudden.

'Stop what?'

'Stop staring.'

'I'm not—' Alice began.

Ed rolled over. The duvet fell off.

'Stop staring at me,' Ed said.

'I wasn't staring.'

'You were.'

'I was looking,' Alice said.

He put his face right up to hers.

'Same difference,' Ed said.

'No,' Alice said. 'Not the same. Looking is just – is just –' She stopped.

'See?' Ed said. 'Can't tell the difference. What would you know, anyway? What would you know about words?'

Alice shut her eyes. Then she rolled on to her back and sat up.

'What are you doing?' Ed said.

Alice didn't open her eyes. 'Getting up.'

'Why?'

'Because,' Alice said, 'it's morning.'

She swung her legs out of bed.

'You woke me,' Ed said.

Alice opened her eyes. She looked down at her bare feet on the floor. In the summer, she painted her toenails pink, but they were bare now.

Ed put a hand on her back.

'Come to bed.'

Alice stood up. She still had her back to Ed. His hand slipped off.

'It's too late,' she said.

'No,' he said, 'it won't take too long.'

Alice began to move towards the door to the landing.

From the bed, Ed shouted, 'You woke me up!'

Alice went through the door, and shut it behind her.

In the bathroom, she ran water into the basin. Then she pulled her hair back into a clip and washed her face with some stuff in a tube, orange stuff that Becky had brought home. Becky was fourteen. She filled the bathroom with beauty stuff and then never used it. Alice used it instead, pink stuff, orange stuff, white stuff.

'I can't bear waste,' she said to Becky.

'I can,' Becky said. She was reading a magazine Alice knew was called *Heat* because people bought it in Mr Chandra's shop, where Alice worked. 'I can bear it with no trouble. Easy.'

Alice looked at her wet face in the mirror above the basin. There was orange stuff sticking to one eyebrow.

4

I am thirty-eight, Alice thought. Thirty-eight. I have a husband and a son and a daughter and a job.

She rubbed at the orange stuff with a towel.

I am lucky, Alice thought. I am lucky to have a family and a job.

She looked at her face again. She knew it so well she could hardly see it. She was very tired of it, too.

But I don't feel lucky, Alice thought. I don't feel lucky at all. I feel—

Someone banged on the door.

'Mum!' Craig shouted.

Alice stared at the mirror.

'Mum!'

I feel forgotten, Alice thought. Forgotten.

'Mum!' Craig yelled.

Like, Alice thought, something that fell down the back of the sofa. And got lost. That's what I feel like.

She went across the bathroom and opened the door. Craig stood outside. He was bare-chested and wearing track pants.

'Don't be so rude,' Alice said.

'You were bloody ages—'

'Don't swear,' Alice said.

5

Craig looked at her. He was now much taller than she was. He was going to look like Ed. In fact, he looked like Ed already.

'You're making me late,' Craig said rudely.

'For school?'

Craig looked amazed.

'Nah,' he said, 'I'm meeting Scott.'

'Craig,' Alice said, 'I don't like you seeing Scott.'

Craig pushed past her into the bathroom.

'You can't stop me,' Craig said, and slammed the door.

# CHAPTER TWO

Mr Chandra's shop was on the corner of Alice's street. It took her two and a half minutes to walk there. Mr Chandra and his wife and his brother worked in the shop seven days a week from seven in the morning till ten at night. Sometimes, they worked till midnight.

When Craig was seven and Becky was six, Alice told Ed she wanted a job. Ed was reading the paper.

'A job?' he said. He laughed. 'Who'd have you?'

Alice was ironing. She folded a sheet and pressed on it. 'The shop.'

'What shop?'

'The corner shop.'

Ed put the paper down. 'Where the new Pakis are?'

'They're not Pakis,' Alice said, 'they're Indian.'

'So,' Ed said. 'They can't read English either.'

Alice pressed down on the sheet very hard. 'Mr Chandra says I can have a cleaning job.'

'What's wrong with cleaning here?'

'After I've cleaned here,' Alice said.

Ed looked at her. 'I don't want you cleaning a Paki shop.'

Alice picked up another sheet. 'I've said yes.'

'Then say no!'

Alice pressed down on the second sheet. 'I said I've said yes.'

Ed got up. His face was red.

He said, 'Well, maybe it's all you're fit for.'

Alice took a deep breath. She ironed very hard, very slowly. Ed went out of the room and, a little later, she heard the door slam.

That was eight years ago. For eight years, Alice had cleaned the shop, washing the floor, wiping the shelves, shining the windows. For eight years, she had learnt, by shape and colour, which the packets of rice were, which the boxes of poppadoms, which the jars of curry paste. She had learnt which chocolate bar was which. She had learnt which newspaper was which. She had learnt what to do with numbers.

Mr Chandra did not teach her.

'Ladies,' Mr Chandra said, 'don't need to know.'

Mrs Chandra could read and write in Bengali, but not in English. She used English for speaking only.

'She does not need,' Mr Chandra said. 'I need. I know.'

Mr Chandra read English newspapers and, when he thought no one was looking, girlie magazines. He was in charge of the money. He took it to the bank, five days a week. His brother was a silent man. He had a limp. He did what Mr Chandra told him.

Mrs Chandra was very noisy. She was in the shop, shouting at customers, or in the house, shouting at her children. She cooked, all day, big pots of red and yellow food. She gave food to Alice sometimes.

'Eat! Eat! You are like a stick insect.'

Alice liked the Chandras. They worked her hard and they paid her badly, but they did not speak to her as if she was a fool. They spoke to her as if she was one of the family. Mr Chandra gave her her money every Friday, out of the till. The bank notes were always dirty.

There was always something the matter with

the Chandra children. They were ill, or they were unhappy, or they were naughty.

'The children,' Mrs Chandra said. 'The children will turn my hair from black to white.'

Alice was cleaning a shelf where the tins stood. Tins of soup, tins of beans, tins of fish and fruit.

'I'm worried about Craig,' Alice said.

Mrs Chandra looked up. 'Your Craig? Such a handsome boy.'

'He's got a bad friend,' Alice said.

Mrs Chandra waved her hand. 'Oh, that will pass. We all have bad friends. It is exciting to have a bad friend.'

'This friend,' Alice said, 'is making Craig rude. He's called Scott. He's got rings and studs everywhere and I'm worried about drugs.'

Mrs Chandra looked alert. 'Talk to the boy's father. At once.'

'It's not so easy—'

'Why not?'

'Because,' Alice said, and then she stopped.

'Because what?'

Alice put down her cloth.

She said, in a small voice, 'Because Craig's

father doesn't think I know anything. He thinks I make things up.'

'Why?' demanded Mrs Chandra.

Alice looked at her. 'You know why.'

'No, I don't.'

'I can't—' She stopped again, and took a deep breath. 'I can't – read very well.'

Mrs Chandra looked amazed. 'What has that got to do with anything?'

'Everything,' Alice said. 'Everything. It makes me – different.'

'What you need to read for?'

Alice shrugged her shoulders. 'Everything,' she said again.

Mrs Chandra leaned forward. 'Why doesn't he teach you?'

'Oh,' Alice said, 'he couldn't do that.'

'Why not?'

'Because – it isn't his fault.'

'Not his fault?'

Alice picked up a tin of soup. 'No,' she said, 'it's not his fault. I was like this when I met him and he still married me. It's not his fault. It's mine.'

There was a silence.

Then Mrs Chandra said, in a very loud voice,

11

'You are mad. Quite mad.'

Alice put the tin on the shelf. 'Yes,' she said. 'That's what Ed thinks I am. And that's what Craig is starting to think I am, too. So why should they listen to me?'

# CHAPTER THREE

BECKY DIDN'T LIKE Alice working in the Chandras' shop. Becky had two great friends, Sara and Zoë. Sara's mother worked in a bingo hall and Zoë's mother was a hairdresser. She went round all the local old people's homes and cut the old men's hair and curled the hair of the old ladies. She said it was lovely work; even if some of the old people were too gaga to talk, at least they weren't cheeky. Sara's mum said the bingo hall was like a party every night.

Becky didn't know what Alice thought about working in the shop. She never asked her.

'She's just helping out,' she told Sara and Zoë. 'She's like that. Always helping people. Drives me nuts.'

Sara and Zoë thought Alice was fine. A bit quiet, perhaps, but no trouble. Sara sometimes said she wished her mother was a bit quieter. More like Alice. She said her mum behaved as if home was a bingo hall too.

'She's that loud,' Sara said, 'she's mental. Can't even read the newspaper to herself. Has to shout it out to the whole world.' She eyed Becky. 'At least your mum doesn't deafen you when she's just reading the bleeding *paper*.'

Becky looked away. She looked at the trees on the edge of the playground.

'No,' Becky said, as if she hadn't really heard. 'No. She doesn't do that.'

'And she didn't create when you dyed your hair.'

Becky said, still looking at the trees, 'I didn't let her see the packet.'

'My mum would have gone spare,' Zoë said. 'My mum wants to know every little last thing about me.'

'I told her,' Becky said, 'that it was shampoo.'

'And she believed you?'

Becky said nothing.

'You are so mega lucky,' Sara said. She undid two buttons on her school shirt. Then she said, in a different voice, 'That's your Craig over there.'

Becky stopped looking at the trees. 'Oh. Yeah.'

Zoë said in an awed voice, 'He's with Scott Miller.'

'Scott Miller,' Sara said, 'is so hot. He is just so hot.' She looked at Becky. She said, 'Has he been round to yours?'

'Not while Mum and Dad are there,' Becky said.

Sara giggled. 'He is one bad boy.'

Becky said, in a bored voice, 'He wants a motorbike.'

'Cool!'

'Can you imagine,' Zoë said in a dreamy voice, 'being on the back of a bike with Scott Miller?'

Sara gave Becky a sharp glance.

'I'll kill you,' Sara said, 'if you're on that bike before me.'

'I won't be,' Becky said, 'I'm just the kid sister. He'll drop Craig anyway. He'll drop him soon. He drops everyone.'

They all looked across at the boys. They were smoking. They were leaning against the wall by the school gates so everyone could see them. Becky thought Craig would not have smoked there, without Scott.

'He only comes to ours,' she said, 'for Craig's

computer. They look up about bikes. They look up about bikes for hours. Does my head in.'

Zoë took the clip out of her hair and put it back again, just the same. Doesn't your mum mind?'

'She doesn't know,' Becky said. 'If she knew, she'd tell Craig off and he'd take no notice.' She stopped for a moment and then she said, 'They smoke in there.'

'Weed?' Sara said.

Becky nodded.

'Cool.'

'Wouldn't your mum go spare if she knew?'

'Course,' Becky said.

Zoë found some chewing gum in her pocket. She held it out. 'What would she do?'

'Mum?' Becky said, taking a strip of gum. 'Oh. Nothing. She'd go spare and do nothing.'

The others looked at her.

'Weird,' Sara said.

Becky put the gum in her mouth. 'We don't let her.'

'What do you mean?'

Becky said in her bored voice, 'We don't let her decide things.'

'Why not?'

16

'Well, she can't.'

'Why can't she?' Zoë said. 'Is she mental or something?'

Becky chewed for a bit.

Then she said, 'She doesn't like being in charge.'

'Oh my God,' Sara said. 'Have you got one of those Nazi dads?'

Becky looked at the trees again. 'Sort of.'

'Does he stop your mum working?'

Becky screwed her face up. 'Sort of,' she said again.

'My dad,' Sara said, 'couldn't find his face with his food if mum didn't tell him where it was.'

'My dad,' Zoë said, and put on her father's voice, 'thinks education is really important.'

'Boring,' Sara and Becky said together.

'He nags me to do my homework.'

Becky stuck her hands in her blazer pockets. 'No one ever nags me. Shouldn't think my dad could spell education if you offered him fifty quid.'

'Wouldn't your mum help him, if that's what she likes doing?' asked Zoë.

There was a silence and then Becky said, 'Those boys are going.'

17

They all looked again. Scott was loping through the school gates and Craig was behind him.

'Where are they going? There's afternoon school,' said Sara.

'Round to ours,' Becky said. 'I bet they're going round to ours.'

The others glanced at her. Their eyes were bright.

'What about your mum?'

Becky shrugged. 'I told you,' she said, 'I told you. She won't do nothing.' She began to walk away from the others.

'She can't,' Becky said, almost to herself.

# CHAPTER FOUR

ALICE LET HERSELF into the house. She was used to coming back and finding it empty. She liked it empty. She put the telly on and looked at the birds on the feeder on the windowsill. She liked birds. She knew most of their names and whether they were male or female. She had learnt that from the old man who lived next door.

He was called Alfie. He had grown up in the country and he knew about birds and trees and animals. He sat in his garden for hours, just watching. Sometimes, he sat there in the rain, or the snow. When Alice asked him about the birds, he told her without looking at her. He only, ever, looked at the birds.

When he died, Alice went to his funeral. There were only three people there. Alfie had had no wife, no children, only the birds. When Alice got home, after the funeral, she went out into her garden and said all the names of all the birds, out loud. She felt she was printing them into her mind.

After that, she tried to look after the birds, like Alfie. She put out the seeds and nuts and bits of bacon fat. She put out a dish of water.

Ed said, 'I see. Birds come before family, do they?'

Becky said with a shudder, 'Don't ask me to touch one.'

Craig said nothing. The only birds Craig saw were blonde ones like Karen Simms, whose bust was bigger than her brain.

Alice put the kettle on. She was tired. Ram, Mr Chandra's brother, had spilt a sack of lentils in the shop, and the lentils had rolled everywhere. Everywhere. Alice had swept up lentils for two hours.

Ram had gone very quiet. Mr Chandra yelled at him, in Bengali, and he said nothing. He tried to take the broom from Alice, but she said, 'I'll do it.' He looked at her. He looked so sad.

Alice made tea in her best mug. It was thin white china with a gold rim. Tea tasted better out of that mug. She looked at the clock.

Numbers were easy. One hour and a half before Ed got home. There was time to drink her tea and look at the birds.

She carried her mug to the kitchen window. There was a bang. It was the bang of the back gate. Alice went stiff. Who was coming through the back gate at this hour? She peered out. It was Craig. Craig, who should be at school. And – Alice gave a little gasp – Scott Miller.

Scott was huge. Craig was tall, like Ed, but Scott was taller. And bigger. He was like a big man with a boy's face and his hair was in little black spikes. He had rings in his eyebrows. And a stud in his nose. Even though the school forbade him.

The back door opened and Craig came in. He stared at Alice. 'Mum!'

Alice said, 'You should be at school.'

Scott came in behind Craig. He looked at Alice as if she was mud on his boots. Alice didn't look back.

Craig said, 'We got stuff to do.'

'What stuff?' Alice's voice was high and thin.

'Bike stuff.'

'You haven't got a bike—'

'My bike,' Scott Miller said loudly.

21

'You should,' Alice said, holding her mug hard, 'do that after school.'

Scott Miller leaned forward a little.

He said, 'Don't you tell me what to do, missus.'

Alice went red. Craig stepped towards the table and put his hand inside his school blazer. He pulled out some papers and slapped them on the table.

'What's that?' Alice said.

Scott Miller pushed the papers towards her. 'Read it and see.'

Craig said quickly, 'She doesn't need to do that. She doesn't know about bikes.'

Scott looked at Alice. Then he looked at the papers. He laid one of his big hands on the top paper. 'That's my CBT.'

'Oh,' said Alice.

'That is a legal form,' Scott said. 'That means I can ride a bike on the road.'

'Oh,' said Alice again.

'It's a Compulsory Basic Training form.'

Alice nodded.

'Don't you believe me?' Scott said.

'I—'

'We need to send this in today.'

Craig said, 'We need to catch the post. We need to check something on the Internet.'

Scott was staring at Alice. Alice was looking at her tea.

'I'm going up to turn the computer on,' Craig said.

'Yeah,' Scott said.

'You coming?'

'Yeah,' Scott said.

Craig looked at his mother. He said, 'It's all legit, Mum.'

He went out of the room. Alice waited for Scott to go, too. He didn't move.

He said, 'You don't believe me.'

'I do—'

'You're acting,' Scott said, 'like you don't believe me.'

Alice said in a rush, 'It isn't that—'

Scott picked up the papers. He held them out. 'Read it,' he said. 'Read it and see.'

Alice shook her head. She felt panic in her throat, behind her eyes.

'Why not?' Scott said.

Alice bent her head. She was not, not going to cry in front of this boy.

There was a silence. A long silence.

And then Scott said in a different voice, a soft, scary voice, 'Oh, I get it. You won't read my CBT form, will you, because you can't.' He stopped, and then he said again, 'You can't read, can you?'

# CHAPTER FIVE

'WHAT'S WRONG WITH YOU?' Liz said.

Liz had been Alice's friend for ten years. They had met at a children's playgroup when Becky was four and Liz was one of the helpers.

Alice put sugar in her coffee.

'I'm fine.'

'No,' Liz said. She leaned forward across the café table. 'No, you are not fine. Are you ill?'

'No.'

'Are you eating? You look really scraggy.'

Alice stirred the sugar in her coffee. 'That's what Mrs Chandra says.'

'Well, she's right,' Liz said. 'And I'm right too. I'm right to know you are worrying.'

Alice took a sip of coffee. 'No more than usual.'

'Yes, you are. Is it Ed?'

'No,' Alice said.

'Is it Becky?'

'No,' Alice said.

'Is it Craig?'

Alice said nothing.

Liz said, 'I see.'

'What do you see?'

'It's Craig,' Liz said. 'You're still worrying about Craig and that Miller boy.'

Alice said in a whisper, 'It's the Miller boy.'

'What's he done?'

'Nothing.'

'Has he scared you? Has he touched you? Little sod—'

'No,' Alice said. 'I mean, yes. He hasn't touched me. But – but he scared me.'

Liz put her hand on Alice's arm. 'How?'

Alice waited.

Then she said, in a tiny voice, 'He knows.'

'What does he know?'

'He knows. He guessed.'

'Alice—'

'He guessed I can't—' Alice stopped.

'What?'

'He guessed I can't read.'

'So?'

'He looked at me,' Alice said, 'as if I wasn't fit to walk on. He looked at me as if I wasn't – I

26

wasn't even a person. Even Ed, when he's in a temper, never looks at me like that.'

Liz folded her arms. 'Why should you care what a boy of sixteen thinks?'

Alice looked at her. 'I do.'

'Well, don't.'

'I do. I have to. He's the same age as my son. He'll teach my son to look at me the same way.' She put her hands over her face. She said, 'I can't bear that.'

'Oh, come on, Alice—'

Alice shook her head. 'All my life people have looked at me that way. I keep telling myself it doesn't matter. But it does.'

'Well,' Liz said. 'Do something about it.'

'I can't. It's too late.'

'I'll help you, you stupid cow. *I'll* help you. 'I'll teach you.'

Alice looked at her. She gave Liz a watery smile.

She said, 'Thank you, but I can't. I can't let you. I can't let you know how much I don't know.'

Liz shrugged. 'Suit yourself.'

'Sorry.'

'I don't need your sorry,' Liz said. 'Anyway,

27

remind me. Didn't you ever go to school?'

'Oh yes,' Alice said. 'Hundreds of schools. Dad never kept a job for more than two weeks. Every time he gave up a job, he moved us on. Sometimes I went to school, sometimes I didn't. Mum didn't like it if I went to school. She wanted me to keep her company. We were always in strange places so I was the only person she knew. She had to make meals out of nothing. That's what she did. Made meals and watched telly. She said that me and the telly, we were her best friends.'

'And now,' Liz said, 'you're afraid of Scott Miller?'

Alice pushed her cup away. 'I'm afraid of what he'll say to Craig. About me. I'm afraid of what Craig will think.'

'So, what are you going to do?'

Alice looked away. 'I don't know. Nothing.'

Liz began to pick up her bags. 'Nothing?'

'Yes.'

'So, no change there then. Alice doesn't like something. Alice does nothing about it.'

'I can't.'

Liz stood up. She put her bag over her shoulder. She said, 'Yes, you can.'

'No—'

'Alice,' Liz said in a fierce voice, 'Alice, you can. Just because you can't read doesn't mean you can't think.'

'But no one knows that but me—'

'Then show them,' Liz said.

'It's too late.'

Liz bent down. She bent until her face was very close to Alice's.

Then she said in an angry whisper, 'It's never too late. Give up if you want to, give up and be miserable all your life, if that's what you want. But I'm telling you something, Alice. I'm telling you that I don't want to see you any more like this. I'm tired of being sorry for you. I'm tired of trying to help. I'm tired of being told I don't understand.'

She stood up and looked down at Alice.

'Ring me,' she said, 'when you're sorted. If you don't get sorted, don't bother.'

Then she walked away from the table very fast and Alice heard the café door slam. Alice looked at her hands on the table. They were shaking.

Help, Alice thought to herself. Help. Oh *help*!

# CHAPTER SIX

RAM CHANDRA WATCHED ALICE. He liked her, because she was quiet. She didn't shout, like his sister-in-law shouted. She didn't fight, like his nephews and nieces. She didn't tell him he was a fool, like his brother. She smiled at him in a shy way. She made him feel that, if he was a fool, he was only a little fool. He watched her while she did her work.

Sometimes she said gently, 'Don't stare, Ram.' But she smiled.

He said to her once, 'I am a lonely man.'

She looked at him.

She said, without smiling, 'We're all lonely, Ram.'

'Yes,' he said, 'being lonely makes you afraid.'

She nodded. He could see she was afraid of some things. She was afraid when customers asked her questions. She was afraid of the newspapers and the magazines. She was afraid of the big alarming boy who was her son's friend. The big alarming boy had rings and studs in his face and sometimes he came in to the shop and calmly took a magazine off the rack and did not pay for it. Ram never asked him for money, if he was alone in the shop. He always just let him take the magazine. The magazines he took were always the ones about motorbikes.

Ram knew he was not afraid of the boy. He also knew that he understood about the motorbikes.

He said to Alice, 'That boy.'

Alice said, 'Which boy?'

Ram said, 'You know which boy.'

Alice went red. She was putting cards in the rack, birthday cards, wedding cards, get-well cards.

'He's bad for Craig,' Alice said.

'Because he has rings and studs and steals things?'

'No,' Alice said. Her back was turned to Ram.

'Then why?'

'Because,' Alice said, 'he thinks we are all stupid. Me in particular.'

Ram waited for a moment.

Then he said, 'He has a weakness too.'

31

Alice shook her head. 'Oh no. Not him.'

'Yes,' Ram said. 'Yes. He does.'

Alice turned. 'What?'

'Motorbikes.'

Alice smiled. Then she laughed. *'Motorbikes?'*

Ram limped out from behind the counter. He put his hand on his bad leg.

'How do you think I got this?'

Alice looked at his leg. Then she looked at his face. 'I don't know.'

'Motorbike,' Ram said.

A customer came in. She was an old lady who came every day. She bought two bananas, a newspaper, a packet of biscuits and seed for her budgie. Then a man came in and bought cigarettes. Then two boys, who bought crisps.

When they had gone, Alice said to Ram, 'What happened?'

'I was seventeen,' Ram said. 'I was the baby of the family. I wanted to leave home but every time I tried to go my mother cried. She didn't speak English. She said if I left, she would die.' He looked at Alice. 'I couldn't let her die.'

'No,' Alice said. She was thinking of her own mother.

'But I wanted to be free,' Ram said. 'I wanted

to be free so much that I had a pain here.' He put his hand on his chest. 'I got an idea. I thought that if I learned to ride a motorbike I could be free, sometimes. I could be free, when I rode my bike, so that I would not mind not being free, with my mother.'

'Free,' Alice said. She thought of the birds in her garden, the birds whose names Alfie had taught her. She wondered why she liked watching them so much. 'Free,' she said again.

'So,' Ram said, 'I told my brother. This brother. He said, "I will help you get work so you can buy a motorbike." He gave me a job in his first little shop. He was kind,' Ram said sadly.

'And then?'

'I passed my test,' Ram said. 'I worked so hard to pass my test. I bought my first bike on the never-never. It was a Honda CL50. It was yellow. It was my pride and joy. It was my freedom.' He looked out of the shop window. 'I rode it whenever I could. I rode it faster and faster. Then I crashed it.'

'Oh Ram!'

He stopped looking out of the window. He looked at Alice. 'I crashed it so badly I was in

hospital for seven weeks. I had to learn to walk
again. My family said no more bikes. I said to
myself, no more freedom. So here I am.'

'Oh Ram,' Alice said again.

'I am used to it now,' Ram said. 'I don't think
about it. Or only sometimes. Like when that
boy comes in and takes the magazines. Then I
think not don't do that but why do you do
that? Why do you want that magazine?'

Alice gave a little laugh. 'He wants to show off
to Craig!'

'No,' Ram said.

'Yes—'

'*NO*,' Ram said more loudly. 'No. He wants
freedom too.'

'He has freedom!'

'No,' Ram said. 'He is too young. He wants it
but he isn't ready for it. He has all this energy
here—' Ram put his hand on his chest again.
'And nowhere for it to go.'

'But—'

'You don't know his home life,' Ram said. 'He
can't say. He doesn't know how to say. He only
knows how to act.' He looked at Alice. 'He can't
say. Just like you can't read.' He smiled. 'That's
why he picked on you.'

# CHAPTER SEVEN

ED TOLD CRAIG HE DIDN'T want Scott Miller in the house again.

Craig shouted, 'You can't stop me!'

Ed was mending a fuse. He did not look up. He said, 'I can.'

'You bar him, you can bar me too!' Craig shouted. 'I'll see him somewhere else! I'll leave home!'

'That so?' Ed said, not looking up.

'He hasn't done nothing!' Craig shouted.

'I don't have to give a reason,' Ed said. 'Not liking his face is a good enough reason for me.' He put the plug down.

Craig said, whining, 'He needs to use the computer.'

Ed stood up. 'He can use someone else's.'

Craig looked at Alice. She was stirring something in a saucepan.

Craig said rudely, 'No use asking you.'

'No,' Ed said. 'No use asking her.'

He went across the kitchen and put his hand on Alice's bottom.

'No use at all,' Ed said, and went out of the kitchen.

Alice went on stirring. Craig opened the fridge and then slammed the door so that all the bottles inside clinked. He swore loudly.

Alice said quietly, 'Bring him.'

There was a silence.

'What?' Craig said.

'Bring him,' Alice said.

'But Dad—'

'I know. Not when Dad's here. When I'm here. After school. *After* it.'

Craig said, in a kind voice as if he was talking to an idiot, 'Don't be daft.'

Alice took the spoon out of the saucepan. 'Does he need a bike?'

'Yes, but—'

'Where are you going to find that bike?'

Craig said in a stunned voice, 'On *autotrader*. On *bargainbasement autotrader*.'

'Is that where you get bikes?'

'He wants a Kawasaki,' Craig said. 'Z AV *50*. 50 cc.'

Alice turned round. 'How's he going to pay

for it?'

Craig stared at her. 'Dunno.'

'Steal the money?'

Craig shrugged. 'Dunno.'

'What does his dad say?'

'Hasn't got a dad.'

'Well, his mum then—'

'*She* doesn't care,' Craig said. 'All *she* cares about is her boyfriend.'

Alice came over to the table. She sat down.

She said, 'He needs a job.'

Craig looked at her as if she had two heads. 'What?'

'If he wants to buy a bike, he needs a job.'

'What,' Craig said, 'cleaning a Paki shop?'

Alice stared out of the window.

She said, 'A job in the bike shop. The bike shop in the Parade.'

'They won't touch him,' Craig said quickly.

'Why not?'

Craig looked away. 'He took a bike. For a laugh. He took a bike and they got funny.'

'Of course they did.'

The back door opened. Becky came in with her school bag. Her school shirt was open so far down you could see her bra.

She said, 'What's going on?'

'Nothing,' Craig said.

Alice said, 'We were talking about Scott Miller.'

Becky went a little pink. 'What about him?'

'Dad's banned him,' Craig said.

'He can't!' Becky said.

Alice said calmly, 'He can. But I can take no notice.'

Becky stared at her. 'You!'

'Yes,' Alice said. 'Me.'

Becky dropped her bag on the floor. She put a hand to her open shirt. 'You'll let Scott Miller come here if Dad says he can't?'

Alice nodded. 'Yes.'

'What are you *like*?' Becky said. 'Who'll listen to you?'

'You will,' Alice said. 'If I help you, if I help your friend, you will.'

'Mum—'

'Think about it,' Alice said.

Craig bent a little so he could stare at her face. 'You on something?'

'No,' Alice said.

'You,' Craig said, 'are shit scared of Scott Miller.'

Alice said nothing. She breathed slowly in and out, in and out.

Then she said, 'No, I'm not.'

Craig said, 'I saw you! I saw you! You couldn't look at him. You were going to wet your knickers!'

'But I didn't,' Alice said.

Becky sat down at the table. She looked at her mother. 'Is this to wind up Dad?'

'It has nothing to do with Dad,' Alice said.

'You're bluffing.'

'Try me.'

'What—'

Alice looked at Craig. 'If you bring him here when you should be at school, I'll go to the headmaster. If you bring him after school, you can use the computer.'

Craig and Becky looked at each other.

'You're mental,' Becky said.

Craig leaned forward. 'S'pose Scott doesn't want your help? S'pose he thinks you're pathetic?'

Alice said, 'I'm not interested in that. I don't care about that.'

'What,' Craig said, 'is going on? What is going *on*?'

Alice looked up from the table. She went over to the cooker and picked up the saucepan. 'You'll see,' she said.

# CHAPTER EIGHT

Liz saw Ed across the car park. Or, at least, she saw a big man putting something into the boot of his car and she thought: That's one fit guy, and then she thought: That's Alice's Ed.

Ed slammed the car boot shut. Then he looked up. Liz waved. Ed smiled. He came across the car park.

'Doing the weekly shop?' Liz said.

Ed shrugged his shoulders. 'She doesn't drive.'

'No.'

Ed looked at Liz's legs.

'There's a lot of things,' Ed said, 'she doesn't do.'

Liz said loudly, 'There's a lot of things she could do if she wanted.'

Ed shifted his gaze from Liz's legs to her face. 'You seen her lately?'

Liz looked away. 'No.'

'I thought,' Ed said, 'that you two were best mates.'

'We had a bit of a bust-up,' Liz said.

'What about?'

'None of your business.'

'What about?' Ed said again.

Liz sighed. 'I offered to help her about something and she refused.'

'Typical.'

Liz said nothing.

'You think,' Ed said, 'that she wouldn't say boo to a goose. Then she goes all stubborn.'

Liz looked Ed straight in the eye. 'She's worried.'

'She's always worried—'

'No,' Liz said, 'she's worried about Craig and this Miller boy.'

'Oh,' Ed said. He smiled and pushed his chest out just a little. 'I sorted that.'

'You did?'

'I banned him,' Ed said. 'I told Craig he was banned. End of story.'

Liz waited a moment and then she said, 'If you say so.'

Ed grinned. 'I do. What I say in my house goes. Alice, Craig, Becky.' He grinned again. 'Want a coffee?'

Liz looked at him. 'No thank you.'

He shrugged again. 'Suit yourself.'

'I do.'

'But make it up with Alice. She hasn't got many friends. In fact, she hasn't got any friends. She can't do with losing you.'

Liz took her car keys out of her pocket and jangled them.

'She knows what she has to do,' Liz said, 'if she wants me back.'

Ed parked the car on the concrete strip beside the house. He got out and opened the boot and yelled for Alice. The deal was that she told him the shopping list, he did the shopping (and changed the list) and she put the shopping away. The deal suited Ed. It gave him control.

In fact, control was one of the things he had liked about Alice in the first place. He'd seen her in a park, with her mum, feeding the ducks on the pond with bread. He noticed her because she was small and blonde, just as he liked girls to be. When he spoke to her mum – he knew it was best to speak to the mother first – Alice had gone pink, and looked away. He liked that too. He liked her shyness. When he got to know her, and discovered she had hardly been to school, he liked that even more. It made her more his, somehow. It put her in his power.

He crossed the concrete strip and opened the back door.

He yelled, 'Alice!'

There was silence. Her handbag was on the table, exactly as he had told her not to leave it. Anyone could walk in and take it, couldn't they? And Craig's school bag was on the floor. But there was no one.

He crossed the kitchen and went into the hallway.

'Alice!'

Silence still. The house was quiet, but strangely quiet. As if it was listening to him. Ed looked in the front room. No one. He went up the stairs. All the bedroom doors were open, except Craig's. Craig's door was shut. Ed went across the landing and opened Craig's door, without knocking.

Inside, Craig's computer was on and in front of it, on two bedroom chairs, sat Craig and Scott Miller. Behind them, leaning towards the screen, over their shoulders, stood Alice. When Ed opened the door, they all three turned round, and looked at him.

44

'Bloody hell!' Ed shouted.

Craig said nothing. Scott Miller said nothing.

Alice said, 'I told them they could.'

'You *what*?'

'I told them,' Alice said, 'that they could look up about bikes on Craig's computer if I was here, but not if I wasn't. And I'm here.'

'How dare you!' Ed shouted.

'They're not smoking,' Alice said. 'They're not nicking stuff. They're looking at *autotrader*. They're looking up about bikes.'

Ed was shaking. 'I banned that little sod!'

Scott Miller went red. He clenched his hands into fists.

'Don't call him names,' Alice said. Her voice shook, but she didn't stop. 'He only wants a bike.'

Ed glared at Alice. 'I want you downstairs.'

Craig looked at his mother. 'You OK?'

She nodded.

Ed jabbed a finger at Scott Miller. 'I want him out!'

Scott stood up, very slowly.

'Now!' Ed shouted.

Scott looked at Alice.

She said, 'You go.'

45

'Now!'

Alice put a hand out. She just touched the sleeve of Scott's sweatshirt. He looked down at her hand. Then he moved his arm away.

'You go,' Alice said, 'but I'll see you next week.'

'You bloody won't!' Ed said.

Craig stood up too. They all stood there, all three males so much taller than Alice. Then Craig moved his head and looked at Scott. Both boys slipped out of the room.

Ed looked at Alice. 'How could you? How could you make a fool of me like that? How dare you?'

Alice looked back at him. He saw her eyes widen. They always widened when she was afraid. Good, Ed thought. Good. She's afraid.

'I didn't make a fool of you,' Alice said. 'I didn't need to. All I'm making is a friend of that boy.'

'What?' Ed said. 'A *friend*? Of crap like that?'

Alice went past Ed to the door of Craig's room. Then she stopped and turned.

She said to Ed, 'I need him,' and then she went downstairs.

# CHAPTER NINE

ON FRIDAYS, MR CHANDRA gave Alice her money in cash. He opened the till and sorted out all the dirty notes and some coins, and then he put the money into Alice's hand. No bag, no envelope, just the dirty notes and coins crumpled into her hand.

When she got home, she counted what he had given her. She was proud of her counting. Mr Chandra nearly always gave her too little. Not much too little, just a bit. A pound or two. Sometimes three. On Mondays, she would tell Mrs Chandra and Mrs Chandra would scream at Mr Chandra and Mr Chandra would give Alice the extra money, very, very slowly as if it hurt him.

When Alice had counted her money, she put it all in her purse to spend on the family, except for a few pounds. Some weeks it was one. Some weeks it was as much as three. She took these saved pounds upstairs to her bedroom. Under the rug that covered most of the floor was a loose board. Alice rolled the rug back, and lifted the board with a spoon handle.

In the space under the floor was a narrow black box. It had once had a bottle of whisky in it, which Ed had been given one Christmas by his boss. Now it held Alice's money, Alice's savings. She did not know what she was saving for, she just knew she had to save. It was another secret, but a happy secret this time. When she walked across the bedroom floor, she knew she was walking across her money.

There was more than three hundred pounds in the whisky box. It had taken Alice nearly four years to save it. When she reached five hundred pounds, she told herself, she would spend it. She didn't know what on. She just knew that five hundred pounds was her goal.

The money was almost all in five-pound notes. Every two weeks or so, Alice would give Mr Chandra five pound coins and ask for a note in exchange. Mr Chandra liked pound coins. He thought Alice didn't like them because they were heavy to carry.

The notes in the whisky box were clipped together, ten at a time. Alice counted them carefully, over and over. Each bundle had ten notes in it. There were nearly seven bundles. Alice took them out of the box and laid them on the rug. Three hundred and forty pounds. And three pound coins.

Alice looked at her money. She picked up each bundle and made sure there were ten blue-green notes in each one. Then she put them back in the box and put the box back in the hole in the floor. Then she rolled back the rug. Three hundred and forty-three pounds. Her money. All her own.

She went across to the chest where she kept her T-shirts and her tops. There was a mirror on the wall above the chest. Alice looked at the mirror.

I have some money, Alice thought, looking at herself. I can buy something. I can buy something I want.

She looked in the mirror at the reflection of the room behind her. She could see the bed, with the dirty patch on the wall, the dirty patch left by Ed's head.

Something strange was happening. She was still afraid of Ed, but not like she used to be. When, the other day in Craig's room, she thought he might hit her, she had not been afraid. She thought: If he hits me, I'll go to the police.

That surprised her. She had never thought that before. She had thought that what Ed and she did was so private, it was another secret. But her ideas about secrets were changing. Her ideas about what was important were changing. That changed what she was afraid of.

'All I'm afraid of now,' Alice said to her own face in the mirror, 'is that he'll try and stop me.'

# CHAPTER TEN

SCOTT MILLER WAS LEANING against a wall. He was watching Craig's sister, Becky. Becky knew he was watching her and she was playing up, laughing too much, showing off her legs.

Scott thought Becky was quite fit. For someone's sister. But she was too young. Scott told himself he didn't like them too young. They got in a state when they were young. Hung around you like a puppy. Then cried. Scott couldn't stand girls crying.

He thought he would just watch Becky and make her think he liked her. He did like her, but not enough to make a move. Just enough to keep in with her, with her family. Her family, Scott thought, were useful to him.

Funnily enough, apart from Craig, it was the mother who was useful. Scott wasn't used to mothers like that, quiet mothers who you thought you could shove around. But you couldn't.

Scott's own mother shoved everyone around all the time. Except the men. She let the men do what they wanted. As long as they stayed. Scott thought women were like that. He thought that all they wanted was a man.

But Craig's mother wasn't like that. In Craig's bedroom, his mother had stood up to his father and his father was a big man. A big man who could read. Craig's mum couldn't read, Scott knew that.

He knew. He knew because, not long ago, he couldn't read either. He started bunking off school when he was seven and he got to fourteen and he couldn't read. Or, at least, he could only read kid stuff.

And then he saw this bike. It was such a bike. It was in the window of the shop on the Parade and Scott leaned on the glass and gazed and gazed at it. He wanted it so badly he had a pain. He had never wanted anything so badly in his life.

Andy, who ran the bike shop, came out. 'Get off!' he shouted.

Scott didn't move. He couldn't move. He couldn't move away from looking at that bike.

'Dream on,' Andy said.

Scott said nothing.

'The likes of you,' Andy said, 'have no more hope of riding that than flying to the moon.'

Scott turned his head, very slowly. 'Why not?'

'Because,' Andy said, sneeringly, 'you have to pass a test, a Compulsory Basic Training test, and you can't even read and write, can you?'

It was Andy's father who took pity on Scott. Andy's father had been a teacher, in a primary school in the country. He kept the books in the bike shop, for Andy, and he saw the look on Scott's face. Over one long winter, he taught Scott to read and write. That was why he and Andy were so angry when Scott took a bike for a joy ride. Without asking.

Scott kicked the wall he was leaning against. He'd been so fed up that day, fed up with his mum, fed up with her boyfriend, fed up with school, fed up with having no freedom. He thought if he just took a bike and let rip for an hour, he'd stop wanting to hit things. He was going to bring it back. He did bring it back.

Becky turned and said over her shoulder, 'Coming to ours later?'

Scott shrugged. He felt fed up again. He knew

the bike he wanted. He knew all he had to know for the test. But he had no money. No money at all. And he needed six hundred pounds.

He slammed his fist into the wall behind him.

'Ouch!' Becky said.

Six hundred pounds! The seller would take half down and half in payment later. But even three hundred pounds was hopeless. Hopeless. Scott peeled himself away from the wall and stood up.

Becky pretended not to notice. She turned her back. Scott went past her, very slowly, and across the playground and out of the school gates. It was not time for the end of school.

There was no one in the road outside. Early afternoon, all empty. Scott scuffed along, kicking at stones. He turned a corner, went down another street. And another. At the far end of the street was the Paki shop where Craig's mum worked. Scott decided he would go in and take a bike mag. If he couldn't have a bike, at least he could look at the pictures.

Mr Chandra was in the shop. Alice was on a ladder, cleaning the top shelves.

Mr Chandra was telling Alice what to do.

'No, not that way. Move those boxes, clean

54

behind, replace. Move *those* boxes, clean behind, replace. If you take that magazine,' Mr Chandra shouted suddenly, 'you will have to pay for it!'

Scott turned. He was holding the magazine.

'Ain't got no money,' Scott said.

'Then put it back!'

Alice said, from the top of her ladder, 'I'll pay for it.'

'You!' Mr Chandra said.

Scott stared at her.

'You're mad,' Mr Chandra said.

Alice came carefully down her ladder. She stood behind Scott. She looked very small.

'Take it out of my wages,' Alice said.

'This boy,' said Mr Chandra in disgust, 'is a waste of space.'

Alice looked up at Scott. She did not look afraid.

She said, 'He'll pay me back.'

'I ain't got no money,' Scott said again.

'No,' Alice said. 'Not in money.'

# CHAPTER ELEVEN

ALICE TOLD ED THAT the lamp in the bedroom wasn't working.

'Change the bulb,' Ed said.

'I did,' Alice said. 'It's not the bulb.'

Ed was reading the sports page in the paper. 'Change the fuse,' he said.

'Please—'

'Please what?'

'Please look at the lamp—'

Ed glanced up. 'Why?'

Ed gave her a long look. 'So you can read in bed?'

Alice said nothing. She turned away. Her head was bent. Ed thought she might be crying. 'You crying?'

'No,' Alice said.

Ed got up. He came and stood behind Alice. He put a hand on her back. She moved away.

'I am not crying,' Alice said. Her teeth were clenched. 'And I've had enough. If you won't mend the lamp, I'll ask Roy next door.'

'No, you won't!' Ed said.

'Then mend the lamp.'

Ed walked round Alice and peered at her face. 'What's got into you?'

Alice looked out of the window. 'I've come to my senses.'

Ed laughed. He said, 'That'll be the day!'

And then he saw Alice's expression. She did not look afraid. She looked as if she just didn't care. Ed felt a small twinge somewhere near his heart. He said, 'I'll mend the lamp.'

Alice stared straight ahead. 'Thank you.'

'I'll mend the lamp now.'

Alice moved away to the table. She picked up her bag. 'I'm going to work.'

'But it's Saturday!'

'I'm working extra hours,' Alice said.

'Why?'

Alice went to the door and opened it. 'Because I want to.'

'Look,' Ed said loudly. 'We don't need the money—'

'You don't,' Alice said and went out and shut the door behind her.

Ed moved to go after her. Then he stopped,

his hand on the door handle. He could shout after her again, but he had a nasty feeling that she would go on walking. That she wouldn't care. He could shout all he liked and she wouldn't hear him.

This made Ed feel very bad. Not bad angry, but bad unhappy. And he wasn't used to feeling unhappy. He walked slowly away from the door, and through the kitchen to the hall. In the cupboard under the stairs, Ed kept his toolbox. He took it out and carried it upstairs.

The broken lamp was on the chest by the bed. Ed checked the bulb. Then he changed the fuse. Then he plugged the lamp in and switched it on. Nothing happened.

Ed sighed. He was good at electrics. He was good with anything to do with how things worked – cars, machines. At school, his wood-work teacher had told him he had a good, practical brain.

'What's practical?' Ed had asked.

'Workable,' the woodwork teacher said. 'You understand how things work.'

Things, yes, thought Ed now. Women, no. Alice, definitely not.

He got down on his hands and knees to

unscrew the socket in the wall. He was beginning to think he had no idea how Alice worked. Or maybe she had changed. Maybe she was working in a different way now.

The floor under Ed's left knee felt strange. As if there was a board missing. As if there was a gap. He pulled back the rug. One board looked as if it didn't fit properly. It looked smaller than the others.

Ed put the tip of his screwdriver into the gap beside the small board, and levered it up. It came up very easily. Underneath there was a space. And in the space was a long black box. Ed knew the box. It was the box he had once had a Christmas bottle of whisky in.

He picked up the box and put it on the floor. Then he opened it. Inside were several little bundles of five-pound notes, and a few coins. Ed took the notes out of the box, and laid them on the floor. Very slowly, he counted them. Three hundred quid. Three hundred and forty quid. All in little bundles, clipped together. Very neat. Very secret.

Ed sat back on his heels. He felt sick. He shut his eyes. There was only one person this money could belong to, and that was Alice. Alice was hiding money under the floor. Alice had money she didn't want Ed to know about. What, Ed wondered, was she going to do with the money? Why was it a secret?

He looked at it again. He had a lump in his throat. He didn't know if he was angry or sad. Was she planning to leave him? Well, if she was, she wouldn't get far. You couldn't get far on three hundred pounds. He put an arm up and blotted his eyes. He hadn't had tears in his eyes for years and years.

Downstairs, a door banged.

Becky shouted, 'Mum!'

Ed quickly picked up the money and put it back in the box. Then he put the box back under the floor and put the board down and rolled back the rug.

The bedroom door opened.

'Where's Mum?'

'Working,' Ed said.

Becky stared at him. 'What are you doing?'

Ed bent his head. Becky mustn't see his red eyes.

'Mending a lamp,' Ed said.

# CHAPTER TWELVE

'THAT BOY,' SAID Mr Chandra.

Alice went on dusting.

'Why,' Mr Chandra said, 'why are you taking his part?'

'He isn't all bad,' Alice said.

Mr Chandra was checking the paper-round list.

'There was a lady in the paper,' Mr Chandra said. 'She was a teacher. She was in court because she had made love with a boy in her class who was sixteen. Sixteen only!'

Alice went red.

'I know the law,' Mr Chandra said. 'I know the law of this country. At sixteen, a boy can leave school and take a wife and buy a lottery ticket. He also can have sex. If he agrees.'

Alice stopped dusting. She turned round. Mr Chandra was looking at her over his spectacles.

'This,' Alice said, 'has nothing to do with sex.'

'My wife—'

'Nothing,' Alice said again, more loudly. 'Nothing. I am – I am not *interested* in sex.'

Mr Chandra shook his head. 'That is very sad.'

'It has to do with motorbikes. And freedom.'

'He cannot ride a motorbike until he is seventeen. It is the law of this country.'

'He knows that.'

'But why,' said Mr Chandra, 'should *you* help him? Why you?'

'He's Craig's friend.'

Mr Chandra shook his head again. 'Small reason.'

'I don't have to give you a reason.'

Mrs Chandra came in through the door to the living quarters. She had been listening.

She said, loudly, 'This is a respectable shop.'

Alice looked at her. Her eyes were very bright.

She said, 'And I am a respectable person.'

The Chandras looked at one another. Then they looked at Alice.

Then Mr Chandra said again, 'This boy—'

Alice put her chin up. High up. She said, 'When I can tell you, I will tell you. There is nothing bad going on.'

Then she walked across to the magazine rack and took down two bike magazines.

'I want to buy these, please.'

Mr and Mrs Chandra stared at her. 'For—?'

'Yes,' Alice said. 'For Scott.'

Alice waited by the school gates. There was a group of mothers by the gates, so she stood back, under a tree. She watched all the children come out, the young ones first, then the big ones. The big ones came slowly, most in groups, one or two alone. There was no sign of Becky. There was no sign of Craig, or Scott Miller. Alice held the magazines and waited.

She waited for ten minutes. Then fifteen. Then twenty. There were no children coming out of school now. The playground was empty. She looked at her watch. No one would be coming now. She would have to go home.

She turned to walk back down the street. There was someone sitting on a wall ten yards away, watching her. It was Scott Miller. He did not move.

Alice walked up to him. 'What are you doing?'

'Same to you,' Scott said. He didn't stand up.

Alice held out the magazines. 'I got you these.'

He looked at them. He didn't take them.

He said 'Why?'

Alice looked round. The street was empty, but there were windows all down it.

She said, 'I've got something to ask you.'

'Yeah?'

'Can we go somewhere to talk?'

Scott still didn't move. Alice looked up and down the street again, and then she sat on the wall too, a long way from Scott. She put the magazines on the wall between them. She said, 'When are you seventeen?'

There was a silence. And then he said, 'Next month.'

'So you could ride a bike then.'

Scott snorted. Alice looked away from him, across the street to a house with a yellow door and a caravan in the garden. She said, 'When did you learn to read?'

There was another silence, and then Scott said, 'Last year.'

'Did it take a long time?'

Scott said nothing.

Alice turned her head and looked at him. 'Did it?'

He nodded.

'Was it hard?'

He nodded again.

'But if it was last year,' Alice said, 'you remember how to do it?'

Scott kicked the wall. 'What's it to do with you?'

'I've got a plan,' Alice said.

'Don't want to hear it—'

'Do you want a bike?'

Scott kicked the wall again.

'Listen,' Alice said. 'Listen. Nobody need know about this but you and me. I've got some money. Every week, I've saved some money. I've got enough now for the down payment on your Kawasaki.'

She looked at Scott. He was quite, quite still. His fingers were gripping the wall and they were white.

'I will give you that money when your birthday comes,' Alice said. 'I will help you buy that bike. But the money isn't a present. You've got to do something in return.' She stopped, and then she said, 'You've got to teach me to read.'

65

# CHAPTER THIRTEEN

LIZ WAS ON HER way home from work. She was tired. She worked in the office in the hospital, and every day seemed busier than the day before. Some days, she could hardly believe that so many people were ill, that so many people had accidents. Some days, she thought there could be almost no well people left in the world because they were all in the hospital.

She walked down the road from the hospital to the bus stop. In her bag, her phone began to ring. She stopped walking and rummaged in her bag for the phone. She looked at the screen. It said, 'Number not known.' Liz put the phone to her ear. 'Hello?'

'It's Ed,' Ed said.

'Ed?'

'Alice's Ed,' Ed said.

'Oh,' Liz said. 'Is she OK?'

'I don't know,' Ed said. 'That's why I rang. Have you seen her?'

'No,' Liz said, 'not for weeks.'

'Can we talk?' Ed said. 'Can we meet for a coffee?'

Liz sighed. 'I'm tired—'

'Tomorrow?'

'I'm working late—'

'Friday,' Ed said. 'Meet me Friday.'

'I don't know—'

'It's about Alice,' Ed said. 'I swear it. I'm not being funny. I need to talk to you about Alice.'

Liz sighed. 'OK,' she said. 'Friday.'

Ed was waiting for her. He had ordered two coffees and put them on the red plastic café table.

'Thanks for coming,' Ed said.

He looked tired, Liz thought. Tired, as if he was worried. He did not look as if he was going to flirt with her.

'It's Alice,' Ed said.

Liz put her bag on the floor. 'What about Alice?'

Ed slumped in his seat. His face looked grey. 'I think she's got a fella.'

Liz stared at him. 'No!'

'She won't let me touch her,' Ed said. 'And she snaps. She snaps my head off.'

'Well,' Liz said, 'you've been snapping hers off for years. And any woman gets sick of being pawed all the time. I do. Some days, I think if Darren touches me, I'll scream.'

Ed took a swallow of his coffee. He said, 'And she's working more.'

'Is she?'

Ed nodded. 'She says she's working Saturdays now. And Mondays.'

'Perhaps she *is* working.'

Ed put down his cup. 'And there's the money.'

Liz looked at him. 'What money?'

Ed looked away. He mumbled, 'I found some money.'

'Were you snooping?'

He shook his head. 'I was mending a lamp.'

'Oh yeah?'

'I was kneeling on the bedroom floor,' Ed said, 'mending a lamp. And the boards felt funny. So I pulled back the rug and found this loose board. And under it was a box of money. Hidden.' He stopped, and then he said bitterly, 'Hidden from me.'

Liz's mouth was open. '*Money*?'

'Three hundred quid,' Ed said. 'All in little bundles. All neat and tidy. All in fivers.'

'Well,' Liz said, 'that wouldn't go far on a fancy man.'

Ed looked at her. He looked as if he might cry.

'It's gone,' Ed said.

'What's gone?'

'The money,' Ed said. 'It was there last week and now it's gone.'

'Did you ask her?'

'No—'

'You big baby. Why don't you ask her?'

'I'm scared,' Ed said.

'Scared?'

'I'm scared she'll say she's bought an air ticket and she's going.'

Liz leaned forward. She tapped on the table with her finger. 'Where would Alice go?'

He shook his head.

'Where,' Liz said, 'would Alice go by herself? How would she manage? She can't even read the departures board!'

Ed sighed. He said, 'I'm sure there's someone.'

Liz sat back in her chair. She looked at Ed. She thought of all the times she had told Alice that

Ed was a bully. Well, he was a bully and, like all bullies, he was weak really, weak underneath. He was weak, and a bully, and he loved Alice. He sat there, big and sad and hopeless because he loved Alice and he was afraid she would leave him. Liz tried not to feel sorry for him but she couldn't help it. He looked so pathetic.

'It's not like Alice,' Liz said.

'But she's different—'

'You mean she's standing up to you.'

Ed shrugged. He said, 'It's more like she can't see me. It's more like trying to catch something slippery. She just slips away.'

Liz leaned forward. She said, 'Why don't you wait?'

'Wait?'

'Why don't you just wait and see?'

Ed said, 'It's killing me, waiting.'

Liz bent to pick up her bag. 'It won't kill you. It might grow you up a bit.'

'Will you see Alice?'

Liz thought a moment. 'I might,' she said. 'I might be quite interested.' She smiled, 'I might get a surprise.'

# CHAPTER FOURTEEN

AT THE BACK OF the bike shop on the Parade, there was an office. It was there that Malcolm, Andy's father, did the books for the business. There was a table and three old chairs and a very old computer. There were piles of papers and boxes of bike parts and a dirty telephone on the wall. It was in this office that Malcolm had taught Scott to read.

Alice looked round the office. It was such a mess.

'It's not the Ritz,' Malcolm said, 'but it's private. No one's going to find you here. No one found Scott.'

Scott stood behind Malcolm. He looked as if he wished he wasn't there.

'I can't do it,' Scott kept saying. 'I can't! I don't know how.'

Malcolm had put some books on the table. They were books Scott knew. One was called *Home Reading*. The others were called *Early*

*Phonics* – *Key Stage 3* and *Phonics Teaching.* Malcolm put his hand on the books. 'You remember these, Scott?'

Scott said, 'I can't teach anyone. I can't, I can't.'

Malcolm looked at Scott. Then he looked at Alice. He was a thin man with glasses and grey hair. He said, 'She'll learn much more quickly than you did. She won't be the pain you were.'

'You teach her,' Scott said. His voice was full of panic. 'You do it! I can't!'

Malcolm smiled. 'I can't.'

He looked at Alice. He said, 'She gave you the money.'

'Take the money!' Scott said.

Malcolm smiled again. 'I can't. It's too late. Andy's in the shop checking your bike right now. Do you want that bike to go back?'

Scott's face was red. He looked as if he might hit someone.

Alice said, 'Just start me off.'

'What?'

'Just start me off. Just show me the letters. Tell me the sounds.'

Malcolm looked at Scott. 'There you are.'

He walked to the door.

Scott shouted, 'Don't go!'

Malcolm said, 'I'll be out there if you need me.'

He walked out and shut the door.

Alice went over to the table. She touched the books. She picked one up. 'What's this?'

Scott didn't move. *'Key Stage 3,'* he said.

'Which is the key word?'

Scott pointed. 'That one.'

'Which one?'

'The first one,' Scott said. 'The little one.'

Alice looked at the word 'key'. She put her finger on the 'k'. 'What sound does that make?'

'K,' Scott said.

'Like cake?'

'Yes,' Scott said.

'And cat?'

'Yes,' Scott said, 'but it's a different letter. It sounds the same but it looks different.'

Alice looked down at the book. 'What does it look like?'

Scott came nearer. He took the book from Alice's hands and opened it. He found a page. 'Like that,' Scott said.

Alice looked at the page.

'Comb, cook, cat,' Scott said.

Alice sat down on one of the wooden chairs. 'Can I write it?'

Scott nodded.

'Will you show me?'

Scott sat down too, not too close. He picked up a pen. He opened the pad of paper Malcolm had left and he wrote 'c c c' on it.

'C,' Alice said. She looked at Scott. 'Craig,' she said, 'Craig has a c.'

Scott wrote his own name down carefully. 'I've got one too.'

Alice looked at his name. She pointed to the s. 'What's that?'

'S,' Scott said.

Alice smiled at him. 'You sound like a snake.'

Scott said, 'Malcolm did that.'

'Did what?'

'When I was learning. He made me make animal sounds. He said—' Scott stopped.

'What did he say?'

'He said I had to listen. I had to learn to listen.'

Alice said, 'I'll learn to listen.'

Scott looked at her. He grinned. 'I had to be a dog. And a frigging cow. And a steam train.'

Alice smiled back. 'What else?'

'I had to act disappointed.'

'Do it,' Alice said.

'Oh-h-h,' Scott said.

'What about not fair?'

'Ah-h-h,' Scott said.

Alice smiled more broadly. 'Can I have a turn?'

'OK,' Scott said.

'Ask me.'

'Growl,' Scott said.

'Gr-r-r-r.'

'Squeak,' Scott said.

'Eek, eek,' Alice said. She was laughing.

Scott leaned forward. 'You got to rhyme stuff,' he said. 'You got to put the jelly in the belly.'

'What else?'

'You got to put the custard in the—'

'Mustard!' Alice said.

'And the fish in the—'

'Dish!'

'And the snake—'

'In the cake!'

The door opened. Malcolm stood there. He looked at them. He smiled. 'I told you,' he said. 'She's not a pain like you.'

# CHAPTER FIFTEEN

CRAIG WAS IN HIS room. The door was shut. Standing outside, Becky could hear games on his computer. They were very loud. They were loud, Becky knew, because Craig was angry and sad. He was angry and sad because Scott Miller didn't come round any more. He didn't come round because he had found a bike, and he had bought it.

'He doesn't need you!' Becky had said, jeering. 'He only ever needed your computer.'

When she had said that she was sorry. Craig looked as if she had hit him. But she didn't know how to say sorry, so she said nothing. And Craig went into his room and shut the door and played loud games on his computer.

At school, Scott Miller kept his distance. He didn't talk to Craig and he didn't look at Becky.

Zoë and Sara said, 'Told you so!'

Sara was going out with a boy from the sixth

form. He had red ears and red hands, but he was a sixth former so Sara didn't care.

'Scott Miller just thinks you're a kid,' Sara said to Becky. 'He won't bother with a kid.'

Zoë said, 'You should have known he'd use you. And then dump you. You should have known.'

Part of Becky had known. Part of Becky knew that she and Craig and their family weren't hard enough or cool enough for Scott Miller. But another part of her thought it couldn't end like that. He couldn't just stop, for no reason. There hadn't even been a row. Scott just stopped coming round and then they heard he had a bike. Where had he got the money from? Had he nicked it?

Craig wouldn't say. He didn't know but he pretended he did, and wouldn't speak to Becky. He wouldn't speak to anyone. He stayed in his room and sulked.

Becky went downstairs. The kitchen was empty. Craig wasn't the only one acting funny. Mum was acting funny too. She was out a lot and she looked – well, she looked happy. And Dad looked like thunder. If Mum looked happy and Dad looked like thunder, Becky thought that something must be going on. Could that something be that Mum was seeing someone?

Becky sat in a chair by the table. She put her arms on the table. Then she put her head on her arms. She didn't know if she wanted to shout or she wanted to cry. What did you do when your family was falling apart?

There was a knock on the glass in the back door. Becky sat up. Mum's friend Liz was outside. She was making faces through the glass.

Becky got up. She opened the door. 'Hi there.'

Liz looked round. 'Where's your mum?'

'Out,' Becky said.

Liz looked at her. 'Is she in the shop?'

'Dunno,' Becky said.

'Well,' Liz said sharply, 'where else would she be?'

Becky thought she might cry.

She said again, in a very small voice, 'Dunno.'

Liz came nearer. She put an arm round Becky.

She said, in a much kinder voice, 'Come on, now. It's your mum we're talking about, remember?'

'Dad's at work,' Becky said. 'Mum's out. Craig won't talk.'

Liz said, 'What about that boy?'

'Which boy—?'

'You know,' Liz said. 'That boy who scared your mother.'

Becky looked at the floor. 'Gone.'

'Well, that's good.'

Becky sniffed.

'Look,' Liz said. 'Your mum wouldn't do anything she shouldn't. Your mum wouldn't say boo to a goose.'

Becky said, 'She said boo to Dad.'

'Yes,' Liz said, 'I know.'

'How do you know?'

'He told me. He's upset. I've never seen your dad upset.'

'I'm upset!' Becky said angrily.

'Why?'

Becky glared at her. 'Where *is* she?'

'Your mum?'

'Yes!'

'I don't know,' Liz said. 'That's why I came round. I told your dad I would. I came round to find your mum and talk to her.'

Becky began to cry. 'Where *is* she?'

There was a sound at the door. Liz looked round. Alice was outside.

'Here,' Liz said to Becky.

Alice opened the door. She was smiling, but when she saw Liz and Becky she stopped smiling and looked worried. 'What's the matter?'

Liz said, 'You tell me!'

Becky glared at her mother this time.

She shouted, 'Where've you been?'

Alice went pink. 'Out.'

'Where?'

'Just out.'

Liz said, 'I think Becky means who were you with?'

Alice put her bag on the table. 'No one.'

'No one!' Becky screamed.

Alice looked at her.

'No one,' Alice said, 'that you need worry about.'

And then she went past them, through the kitchen, and out of the door to the hall.

# CHAPTER SIXTEEN

LIZ WAITED AT THE corner of the street. She stood just behind a big lilac bush which had thick green leaves. If she pushed one branch down a little way, she could see the front of Mr Chandra's shop. She had been watching Mr Chandra's shop for nearly an hour. She was waiting for Alice to come out.

Other people came out all the time. There were customers, and two of the Chandras' children, and Ram, Mr Chandra's brother. He got on a bicycle and rode away up the street, and the Chandra children shouted at him as if he was a stranger.

It was over an hour before Alice came out. Liz looked to see what she was wearing. She was wearing the same clothes she usually wore: black trousers, white top, pink quilted jacket. She'd been wearing those clothes the other day. She *always* wore those kind of clothes. She told Liz once that she had seven white tops for the seven days of the week. Well, Liz thought, if she's meeting a man, he isn't a man who cares about how she looks.

Alice set off down the road. Liz waited two minutes and then she followed her. She kept close to the walls of the houses in case she had to hide. But Alice didn't look back. Alice walked to the end of the road and Liz waited for her to turn towards her own house. But she didn't. She turned the other way.

Alice was walking fast. She crossed two streets and then she turned towards the main road.

Goodness, Liz thought, hurrying behind her. Goodness. Where is she going? To the café?

When she got to the main road, Alice stopped. She looked at her watch. Then she ran a hand through her hair.

If she puts lipstick on, Liz thought, it's a fella.

But Alice didn't put lipstick on. She turned to the left, towards the Parade. She walked past the baker and the newsagent and the flower shop and the betting shop. When she got to the motorbike shop at the end, she stopped. She looked round her, carefully. And then, to Liz's amazement, she went in. She went down the side of the shop and in through a door.

Liz leaned against the wall near by. She felt sick. There could only be one reason for Alice to go in through the side door, only one reason for her to look round like that. She was meeting Andy, from the bike shop. Andy of all people!

All that nonsense with Craig and Scott and the computer and motorbikes, and it had gone to Alice's head. Liz got out her phone. She had promised to ring Ed.

Becky had never followed anyone before. She had to half run to keep up with Scott. If he turned and saw her, she thought she'd die, but she also thought she'd die if she didn't know why he'd stopped coming round. She knew she had to say, 'Is it me?'

She didn't know how she would say it but she knew she had to. 'Is it me?'

Even if he said, 'I never even thought about you,' that would be better than not knowing.

He wasn't walking really, he was loping. Becky scuttled behind him, her eyes fixed on his leather jacket. He went all the way to the main road and then he swung left down the Parade. Becky opened her mouth to call his name, but nothing came. Her mouth was dry. Scott came level with the bike shop and vanished. Becky ran the last yard or two. She saw Scott go in through a side door and heard it slam. She ran up to the door and put her hand on the handle. But she wasn't brave enough. She couldn't do it.

Becky turned away. Stupid, she thought, stupid, *stupid*. What did you think would happen? Did you really think he'd talk to you? Did you really think he'd do anything but laugh at you? At least, she thought, Sara and Zoë don't know how stupid I've been.

'Becky!' Liz said.

Becky's head shot up. 'What are you doing here?'

'Same to you,' Liz said.

Becky's face was hot. 'I was just—' She stopped.

'I know,' Liz said, 'I know. I saw you. You were following that boy.'

Becky said nothing.

'I saw you,' Liz said. 'I saw him. He went in where your mum went in.'

Becky's eyes were wide. 'Mum!'

'Yes,' Liz said, 'yes. Your mum.'

'She went in there. She went in where that Andy works.'

'She can't—'

'She can,' Liz said. Her voice was loud. 'She can.' She put out a hand and gripped Becky's arm. 'And we're going to find out!'

'No—'

'Yes, we are,' Liz said. 'We're going to see what's what and then I'll ring your dad.'

She began to drag Becky down the building towards the side door.

'No!' Becky said. 'No! I don't want to know!'

'I do,' Liz said, 'and you have to. You have to know what your mum is up to.'

She stopped by the door. She was panting and still holding Becky's arm.

'Here we go,' Liz said.

She took hold of the door handle and turned it. The door swung open. Inside they could see a small room with a table and chairs and piles of papers and mess. And at the table, staring at them as if they were seeing ghosts, sat Alice and Scott Miller. And both of them had books in their hands.

# CHAPTER SEVENTEEN

RAM CHANDRA SAID TO Alice, 'You look happy these days.'

Alice was in the shop window with a bucket, to clean the glass. She didn't turn round.

'Happy,' Ram said, 'and not so thin.'

Alice put a rag in the water in her bucket, and squeezed it dry.

Ram said, 'Is it because of that boy? Has he stopped bothering you? He hasn't been in to take a magazine for weeks.'

Alice turned round. She was smiling. 'Yes,' she said, 'it's because of that boy.'

Ram was sorting fruit on the rack. It all looked very tired. 'It's bad,' he said. 'It's bad he frightened you.'

'But he stopped.'

'What?'

'He stopped frightening me. I did what you said. I got to know him.'

Ram turned an apple over so that a brown

spot didn't show. 'You be careful.'

Alice looked at him, still smiling.

'You be careful, with a boy like that.'

Alice turned back to the window. 'Oh,' she said, 'I'm very careful.' She stopped, and then she said in a very low voice, 'And so is he.'

Ed was sitting at the kitchen table. It was after six, and Alice wasn't home. She had asked him that morning if he would look at the washing machine. 'It's leaking.'

'OK,' Ed said. He didn't look at her. It was hard to look at her these days.

'And maybe,' Alice said, 'you could fix the window catch in the bathroom. And have a look at my bird table. The top wobbles.'

'Anything else?' Ed said. He gave her a quick glance. There was a sneer in his voice. 'Why don't you write a list?'

Alice said nothing. Ed looked at her quickly again, to see her hurt face. But her face wasn't hurt. It looked as it looked most of the time these days. It looked almost happy.

When Ed got in from work, he looked at the washing machine. He took a kink out of the hose. Then he put a screw in the window catch.

Then he nailed the bird table. Then he sat at the kitchen table and stared at the paper but couldn't see it.

He looked at the clock. Ten past six. Alice was out, Becky was out, Craig was in his bedroom with the door shut. Ed was hungry. He was also cross and tired and worried and sad. He glanced at the paper.

'Woman wins prize.'

Ed banged the paper.

'I bet she bloody does,' Ed said. 'Women! What about the men?'

The door to the hall opened.

Craig said, 'Talking to yourself?'

Ed grunted.

Craig looked round the kitchen. 'Where's Mum?'

'Dunno.'

'I'm starving,' Craig said.

He went over to the fridge and opened the door.

'Don't,' Ed said.

'Look—'

'*Don't*', Ed said. 'Just don't. Wait for your mother.'

'But—'

'Did you hear me?' Ed shouted.

Craig looked amazed. He said, 'Suppose she doesn't come back?'

Ed said nothing. He stared at the paper.

Craig said, 'Where's she gone, Dad?'

There was silence and then Ed said, as if spitting out the words, 'I don't bloody know.'

There were steps outside. Ed and Craig both looked at the door, like dogs who think they hear their master. The door opened. It was Becky.

'Bloody hell,' Ed said.

Becky looked at her father. 'Charming—'

Ed got up from the table. 'I thought it was your mother.'

Becky gave a little smile. 'Did you now?'

Ed shouted, 'Yes I did! And where the hell is she?'

Becky put her school bag on the floor. Then she went over to the sink and washed her hands, very slowly. Her father and her brother watched her in silence.

Becky turned round. 'Hungry?' she said to Craig.

'What's going on?' Craig said.

Becky looked at them. They were the same

height, but Ed was broader. They looked like two versions of the same person. They looked, at that moment to Becky, like two big, sad, stupid blokes.

She dried her hands, very slowly.

'What's going on?' Craig said again.

Ed said, 'Where is she?'

Becky looked down. She smiled, still looking down. 'She's in the Parade.'

'The Parade?'

'She's in the bike shop.'

Ed took a step forward. He said, amazed, 'But she hasn't got a bike, she couldn't—'

'No,' Becky said, 'she couldn't. She hasn't. But Scott has.'

Craig said, 'Scott?' His eyes were twice their usual size. *Scott?*

'Yes,' Becky said. She looked up and smiled right at them. 'Yes, Mum is in a room at the back of the bike shop. With Scott. She gave Scott the money to put down on a bike.'

'I'll kill her!' Ed shouted. 'I'll kill them both!'

'And in return,' Becky said, taking her time, 'Scott is teaching her to read.'

There was a sudden, complete silence. It was so quiet that Becky could hear her father and brother breathing. They were breathing so hard they were almost panting.

'What?' Ed said at last. His voice sounded tiny and far away. *'What?'*

'Andy's dad taught Scott to read,' Becky said, 'for his bike test. Andy's dad was a teacher. He's got all the books. So Mum said to Scott, if I give you the money for your bike, will you teach me to read. And he is.'

Ed groped his way to the table and sat down. He put his head in his hands. Becky looked at him.

'Sometimes,' she said, 'I don't know why Mum likes you. But she does. And you're such a dork.'

Then she looked at Craig. 'So are you,' she said. 'Must be inherited.'

# CHAPTER EIGHTEEN

ALICE LOOKED OUT OF the kitchen window. There were four tits on the bird table and a sparrow. It was good to see a sparrow. They were rare these days. She had put out seed and crumbs and tied some bacon rashers on a bit of string. The day before, there had been a woodpecker, black-and-white spotted, with a red head, pecking at the bacon.

She turned back to the kitchen. It was very tidy. She had felt the urge to clean and tidy it, to polish the sink, to wash the floor. In fact, she felt the urge to wash all the floors, clean the whole house. And then to go out and have her hair cut. And buy a new top, a top that wasn't white, like all the others.

Alice looked at the table. There was nothing on it except some flowers in a jug, and a newspaper. Ed had brought the flowers. They were pink and purple, a bit squashed, and he had thrust them at her without a word. He looked as shy as a boy on a first date.

'Goodness,' Alice had said, 'what's going on? You never give me flowers.'

Ed mumbled something.

'You last gave me flowers,' Alice said, 'when Becky was born. That wasn't yesterday.'

Ed mumbled again.

'What?' Alice said.

'Sorry,' Ed said, looking at the floor.

Alice cut the stalks of the flowers and put the flowers in a pink jug with water and an aspirin to wake them up. Then she put them next to Ed's paper. It was yesterday's paper, but Alice didn't want to throw it away. She thought that perhaps she would never throw it away. She had looked at that paper when she got home from her lesson and she had seen something. She had looked at the black-and-white shapes and she had, for the first time, seen what they meant.

'Woman wins prize.'

Alice stared at the letters.

'Woman wins prize.'

She remembered what Scott had said when he told her about the first time he rode a bike. 'I was free,' Scott said. 'Nobody could catch me.'

Alice touched the pink and purple flowers with her finger. Then she picked up the newspaper and held it against her, very carefully. Then she shut her eyes.

'Woman wins prize,' she said to herself. She was smiling. There were birds on the bird table and flowers in a clean kitchen and she was holding the key to the future.

'Nobody,' Alice said to the empty kitchen, 'nobody's going to catch me now, either!'

# A NOTE ON THE AUTHOR

Joanna Trollope is the author of a number of historical novels and of *Britannia's Daughters*, a study of women in the British Empire. In 1988 she wrote her first modern day novel, *The Choir*, and this was followed by *A Village Affair*, *A Passionate Man*, *The Rector's Wife*, *The Men and The Girls*, *A Spanish Lover*, *The Best of Friends*, *Next of Kin*, *Other People's Children*, *Marrying the Mistress*, *Girl From the South*, *Brother and Sister* and *Second Honeymoon*. She lives in London and Oxford.

# WORLD BOOK DAY
# *Quick* Reads

We would like to thank all our partners in the
*Quick* Reads project for all their help and support:

BBC RaW
Department for Education and Skills
Trades Union Congress
The Vital Link
The Reading Agency
National Literacy Trust

*Quick* Reads would also like to thank the Arts
Council England and National Book Tokens for
their sponsorship.

We would also like to thank the following
companies for providing their services free of
charge: SX Composing for typesetting all the titles;
Icon Reproduction for text reproduction; Norske
Skog, Stora Enso, PMS and Iggusend for paper/board
supplies; Mackays of Chatham, Cox and Wyman,
Bookmarque, White Quill Press, Concise, Norhaven
and GGP for the printing.

**www.worldbookday.com**

# *Quick* Reads

## BOOKS IN THE *Quick* Reads SERIES

| | |
|---|---|
| *The Book Boy* | Joanna Trollope |
| *Blackwater* | Conn Iggulden |
| *Chickenfeed* | Minette Walters |
| *Don't Make Me Laugh* | Patrick Augustus |
| *Hell Island* | Matthew Reilly |
| *How to Change Your Life in 7 Steps* | John Bird |
| *Screw It, Let's Do It* | Richard Branson |
| *Someone Like Me* | Tom Holt |
| *Star Sullivan* | Maeve Binchy |
| *The Team* | Mick Dennis |
| *The Thief* | Ruth Rendell |
| *Woman Walks into a Bar* | Rowan Coleman |

### AND IN MAY 2006

| | |
|---|---|
| *Cleanskin* | Val McDermid |
| *Danny Wallace and the Centre of the Universe* | Danny Wallace |
| *Desert Claw* | Damien Lewis |
| *The Dying Wish* | Courttia Newland |
| *The Grey Man* | Andy McNab |
| *I Am a Dalek* | Gareth Roberts |
| *I Love Football* | Hunter Davies |
| *The Name You Once Gave Me* | Mike Phillips |
| *The Poison in the Blood* | Tom Holland |
| *Winner Takes All* | John Francome |

**Look out for more titles in the *Quick* Reads series in 2007.**

www.worldbookday.com

**Have you enjoyed reading this**
*Quick* Reads **book?**

**Would you like to read more?**

**Or learn how to write fantastically?**

If so, you might like to attend a course to
develop your skills.

Courses are **free** and available in your local area.

If you'd like to find out more,
phone **0800 100 900.**

You can also ask for a **free video or DVD** showing
other people who have been on our courses and
the changes they have made in their lives.

**Don't get by – get on.**

# FIRST CHOICE BOOKS

If you enjoyed this book, you'll find more great reads on www.firstchoicebooks.org.uk. First Choice Books allows you to search by type of book, author and title. So, whether you're looking for romance, sport, humour – or whatever turns you on – you'll be able to find other books you'll enjoy.

You can also borrow books from your local library. If you tell them what you've enjoyed, they can recommend other good reads they think you will like.

First Choice is part of The Vital Link, promoting reading for pleasure. To find out more about The Vital Link visit www.vitallink.org.uk

## RaW

Find out what the BBC's RaW (Reading and Writing) campaign has to offer at www.bbc.co.uk/raw

## NEW ISLAND

New Island publishers have produced four series of books in its Open Door series – brilliant short novels for adults from the cream of Irish writers. Visit www.newisland.ie and go to the Open Door section.

## SANDSTONE PRESS

In the Sandstone Vista Series, Sandstone Press Ltd publish quality contemporary fiction and non-fiction books. The full list can be found at their website www.sandstonepress.com.

## *Quick* Reads

### *Star Sullivan* by Maeve Binchy

### Orion

Star wanted everyone to be happy. She wanted her father to stop gambling, her mother not to work so hard, her brother to stay out of trouble and her sister to stop worrying about what she ate.

But when Laddy moved in next door, Star changed and was no longer the sweet, thoughtful girl everyone loved . . .

*Quick* Reads

### *The Thief*
### by Ruth Rendell

### Arrow

### What you do in childhood may come back to haunt you . . .

Stealing things from people who had upset her was something Polly did quite a lot.

There was her Aunt Pauline; a girl at school; a boyfriend who left her. And there was the man on the plane . . .

Humiliated and scared, by a total stranger, Polly does what she always does. She steals something. But she never could have imagined that her desire for revenge would have such terrifying results.

'Ruth Rendell knows how to make your hair stand up straight on your head'
Maeve Binchy

## *Quick* Reads

### *Blackwater* by Conn Iggulden

### HarperCollins

*Blackwater* is a cold, dark thriller with a twist.

Davy has always lived in the shadow of his older brother, who will stop at nothing to protect himself and his family. But when Denis Tanter comes into Davey's life, how far will they go to get him out of trouble?

How far can you go before you're in too deep?

## Quick Reads

### *Woman Walks into a Bar*
### by Rowan Coleman

### Arrow

Twenty-eight-year-old single mother Sam spends her days working in the local supermarket and her Friday nights out with her friends. Life has never been easy for Sam, but she's always hoped one day she'll meet the 'The One'.

She's starting to lose hope when her friends set her up on a blind date. At first Sam's horrified, but then she agrees – after all, you never know when you might meet the man of your dreams . . .

# *Quick* Reads

### *Don't Make Me Laugh*
### by Patrick Augustus

### The X Press

It's not funny. Leo and Trevor are twins, but they hate each other's guts. Leo says his brother got off with his woman. Trevor reckons it was the other way round. Only Mum can stop them ripping each other to bits. But HER big secret is that one of them has to die.

## Quick Reads

### *Screw It, Let's Do It* by Richard Branson

### Virgin

**Learn the secrets of a global icon.**

Throughout my life I have strived for success – as a businessman, in my adventures, as an author and a proud father and husband. I want to share the many truths I've learned along the road to success which have helped me to be the best I can. They include:

Have faith in yourself
Believe that anything can be done
Don't let other people put you off
Never give up

Learn these and other simple truths, and I hope you will be inspired to get the most out of your life and to achieve your goals. People will try to talk you out of ideas and say, 'It can't be done,' but if you have faith in yourself you'll find you can achieve almost anything.

*Quick* Reads

*How to Change Your Life in 7 Steps*
by John Bird

**Vermilion**

Want to improve your life but don't know where to start? Then this is the book for you.

John Bird explains his seven simple rules that could change your life. You might want to get a new job, stop smoking or go back to college. This book tells you how you can take what you've been given and turn it into something you'll be proud of.

## Quick Reads

### *Someone Like Me* by Tom Holt

### Orbit

When the hunter becomes the prey . . .

In a world torn apart by hatred and fear, only the strongest survive.

Nobody knows where they came from. Nobody knows what they want. The creatures are killing humans for meat and nobody, it seems, can stop them.

Now one man – a hunter by trade – has trapped one of the creatures. Under the ground they face each other. Only one of them will get out alive.

## Quick Reads

### *Hell Island* by Matthew Reilly

### Pan Books

Welcome to hell on earth.

Hell Island doesn't appear on any maps. It's a secret place where classified experiments have been going on. Experiments that have gone terribly wrong . . .

When all contact with the island is lost, four crack special forces units are dropped in. Their mission: to discover what has happened.

Nothing has prepared them for what they find.